To all the grandpas and grandmas.

Cataloging-in-Publication Data has been applied for
and may be obtained from the Library of Congress.
ISBN: 978-1-4197-0588-5

Text and illustrations copyright © Marta Altés 2012
Moral rights asserted.

First published in Great Britain by Macmillan Children's Books in 2012.

Published in 2012 by Abrams Books for Young Readers,
an imprint of ABRAMS. All rights reserved. No portion of this book may
be reproduced, stored in a retrieval system, or transmitted in any form or
by any means, mechanical, electronic, photocopying, recording, or otherwise,
without written permission from the publisher.

Printed and bound in China
10 9 8 7 6 5 4 3 2 1

Abrams Books for Young Readers are available at special discounts when
purchased in quantity for premiums and promotions as well as fundraising or
educational use. Special editions can also be created to specification. For details,
contact specialsales@abramsbooks.com or the address below.

ABRAMS
THE ART OF BOOKS SINCE 1949
115 West 18th Street
New York, NY 10011
www.abramsbooks.com

marta altés

My Grandpa

Abrams Books for Young Readers, New York

My grandpa is getting old . . .

Sometimes he feels alone.

But then I come along!

When he is with me, he smiles.

When I am with him, I can fly!

At times he behaves like an old man.

At times he's like a child.

Occasionally he doesn't recognize me ...

but my hugs can solve it.

Some days,
I am his eyes . . .

Some days, he is mine.

Together we have traveled the world ...

Although sometimes he gets lost.

My grandpa is getting old . . .

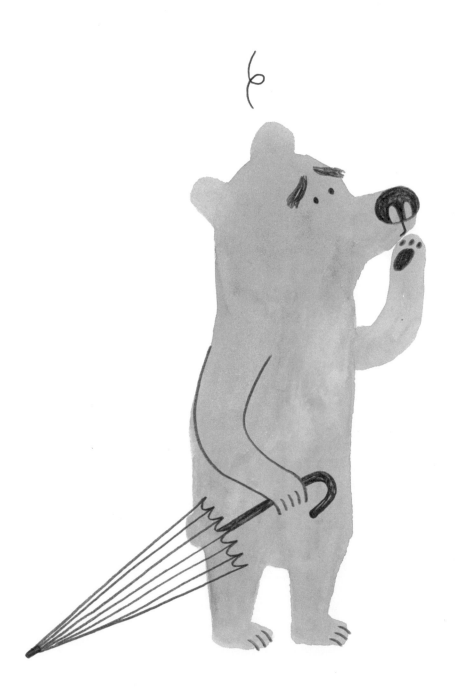

But that's how he is ...

and I love him.